Lily & Baa in PARIS

Created by
Sohanya R. Cheng

Illustrated by
Wing Yee Lee

D1406966

With a hop, a skip and an ooh la la
Off to see PARIS with my sweet Baa
We sing, we jump, and we dance
As we head to Paris.... the capital of France!

The Eiffel Tower looked over downtown
Shaped like a V - but upside down
She stood tall and kissed the sun
I shouted from the top

So down we scrambled like a speeding truck
I really hope we are not out of luck
It danced in the wind like a kite in flight
Over shops and trees - what a sight!

'Look up!' Cried Baa 'it's heading to the triangle'
A pyramid shaped museum with funny little angles
My little red hat told the birds to 'shoo!'
Hiding behind trees, playing peek-a-boo!

"All this running and I'm starving,"

groaned Baa

"For pastries with chocolate—

OH LA LA"

In a nearby patisserie-

that smelled like heaven

I bought us macaroons –

a whole SEVEN!

Baa yawned and it was time to rest
She curled up close onto my chest
It's just a hat – it really doesn't matter
A hug with Baa makes it ALL better.

As the sun set on Paris skies
It was time to say our goodbyes
with a hop, a skip and an ooh la la
Oh Baa, how lucky we are!

Moulin Rouge

Notre Dame

Louvre

Rose Bakery

St. Germain

Séine River

I ♥ Paris

Made in the USA
Lexington, KY
15 December 2016